The Village That Saves
The Toy Convoy

Inspired by True Events

Written and Illustrated by

Katy O Ishee

Printed in the United States of AmericaFirst Printing, 2019

ISBN 9781698824253

Friends in the Wind, PO Box 72, Normandy TN 37360

www.facebook.com/villagethatsavesthetoyconvoy

For extra copies katyishee@mac.com

Dedicated To

Thank you to all of the good people,

who shared with me with their ideas

and for helping me bring this

story to life.

Thanks to all of you who took time out of your

life to help brighten Christmas for the children

who can't help themselves. God Bless You.

In memory of our

brothers and sister

Bear, Sandra and Rocky.

Ride Free in Harley Heaven,

and Ms. Jean and Santa

Long ago and not too far away,
was a little town called Toilethoma,
that welcomed the convoy,
Santa and his sleigh.

People came from miles around
to see the funny rides.
Big ones, little ones, fat ones,
All riding side by side.

There were motorcycles
and hot rods,

Trucks and jeeps

Big horns and little horns
and horns that went beep... beep!

There were black cars,
red ones

White trucks and green.
There wasn't a color
that couldn't be seen.

The American flags
blew in the breeze

Kids along the roadside waved them
to remind us we were free.

For years Santa led the convoy
into that little town,
Children came from all around.

It was something young and old
loved to see.
There wasn't a better place
for you and me.

The cars and trucks were full of toys
They were going to help
good girls and boys.
Bikes, games, and toy guns
made of tin,
They knew these folks
had good hearts
and that they were their friends.

One day a big dark cloud
rolled over Toilethoma,
no sunshine could be found.
The air smelled like skunks
falling from the sky to the ground.

Three rotters climbed
out of the deep black well.
They were selfish and ugly
and their breath really smelled.

They came to run the convoy
out of that little town.
The old stink'n rotters didn't care
it helped children from all around.

15

The rotters hearts
were cold as ice.
Their eyes were evil,
their skin full of lice

Ginny Rotter was mean and ugly,
she looked just like a sow,
and every time she opened
her mouth, she mooed
just like a cow!

Rogue Rotter was crooked.
His big teeth lied to you.
He was always tell'n you,
what you could and couldn't do.

Old Curly Rotter had two faces
veryone knew his heart was blac
And all of that fake kindness
Was just a phony act.

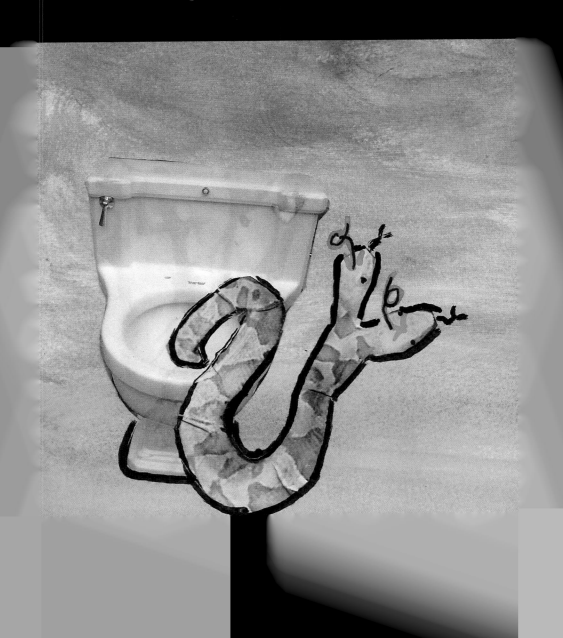

The children cried when they heard
the convoy
would no longer come to town.
The word spread fast throughout the land
a new home had to be found.

There was a kind old gentleman,
by the name of Mr. Nick,
some wondered if he was for real.
Nick lived in the Christmas Village
tucked away in the Tennessee hills.

Nick heard the convoy didn't
have a home,
So he invited them to his Christmas Village,
so they didn't have to roam.

When it was time for the convoy
All of the people with good hearts
Lined up in the convoy,
Excited for it to start.

God was watching from up above
and smiled on the convoy full of love.
He blew the dark clouds away
And gave them a pretty sunny day.

They were going
to the Christmas Village,
Their flags were flying high.
Children were laugh'n and bells tinkled,
when Santa's helpers walked by.

There were motorcycles and hot rods
and the convoy grew.
Longer and bigger than ever,
The skies were sparkling blue.

The people waved when they rode thru Toilethoma. The three stink'n rotters looked the other way. The mean old rotters could see they had not spoiled that special day.

They couldn't spoil that special day
No matter how they tried,
Because everybody knew their stories
were nothing but a pack of lies.

They were going to the Christmas Village,
where children lined the square,
they all waited wide eyed for Santa,
knowing he'd be there.

Everyone waved their flags
when the convoy rode
into town.
And Santa visited with
all the kids
who had gathered all around.

"Thank you, Mr. Nick,
It's the Best Convoy Ever!"

And the mean old rotters
disappeared...
because mean doesn't
last forever.

It's not the end
but a new beginning.

Katy O Ishee

The Village That Saves The Toy Convoy is Katy's 5th book.
Toy Runs have always had a special place in Katy' heart.
She has organized the Highway 41 Toy Convoy for 23 years.
She organized Citrus County's first toy run in 1981
in Inverness, Florida.
Katy married her husband Virgil T at a Toy Run
in Pensacola, 1994,
She loves
writing, painting, motorcycling and listening to Virgil sing.
Her pet peeves are two faced people and liars.

Believe YOU Can!

Made in the USA
Lexington, KY
12 November 2019